PUFFIN BOOKS

Not Quite a
Mermaid
MERMAID ISLAND

Linda Chapman lives in Leicestershire with her family and two Bernese mountain dogs. When she is not writing she spends her time looking after her two young daughters, horse riding and teaching drama.

D0391405

Books by Linda Chapman

MY SECRET UNICORN SERIES
STARDUST SERIES

BRIGHT LIGHTS
CENTRE STAGE

Not Quite a Mermaid

MERMAID ISLAND

LINDA CHAPMAN

Illustrated by Dawn Apperley

PUFFIN

PUFFIN BOOKS

Published by the Penguin Group
Penguin Books Ltd, 80 Strand, London WC2R 0RL, England
Penguin Group (USA) Inc., 375 Hudson Street, New York,
New York 10014, USA
Penguin Books (Canada), 10 Alcorn Avenue, Toronto, Ontario,
Canada M4V 3B2 (a division of Pearson Penguin Canada Inc.)
Penguin Ireland, 25 St Stephen's Green, Dublin 2, Ireland
(a division of Penguin Books Ltd)
Penguin Group (Australia), 250 Camberwell Road, Camberwell,
Victoria 3124, Australia (a division of Pearson Australia Group Pty Ltd)
Penguin Books India Pvt Ltd, 11 Community Centre, Panchsheel Park,
New Delhi – 110 017, India
Penguin Group (NZ), cnr Airborne and Rosedale Roads, Albany,
Auckland 1310, New Zealand (a division of Pearson New Zealand Ltd)
Penguin Books (South Africa) (Pty) Ltd, 24 Sturdee Avenue,
Rosebank, Johannesburg 2196, South Africa

Penguin Books Ltd, Registered Offices: 80 Strand, London WC2R 0RL, England

www.penguin.com

First published 2005
3

Text copyright © Linda Chapman, 2005
Illustrations copyright © Dawn Apperley, 2005
All rights reserved

The moral right of the author and illustrator has been asserted

Set in Palatino
Made and printed in England by Clays Ltd, St Ives plc

British Library Cataloguing in Publication Data
A CIP catalogue record for this book is available from the British Library

ISBN 0–141–31836–8

*To Pippa le Quesne – for giving me the chance
to write in the first place and for being such
a fantastic editor and friend.
Thank you*

Contents

Chapter One

Electra the mermaid swam beside the coral reef and looked out at the small rocky island standing all alone in the deep sea. The waves were breaking against its dark jagged cliffs. 'I wonder what's on that island over there,' she said. 'It looks really exciting.' She flicked back her long red hair and glanced round. 'I bet it wouldn't take me long to swim to it. Do you dare me to try?'

Sam and Sasha, the mer-twins who lived in the cave next door to Electra, stared at her.

'No way,' Sam said, his green eyes widening in alarm. 'You know we're not allowed to go outside the coral reef into the deep sea, Electra.'

Sasha nodded. 'Dad says there are sharks and electric eels and giant squid out there. You could get injured – or even killed – if you tried to swim to the island.'

Electra frowned. 'Electric eels and giant squid are just stories. I've never seen any. And as for sharks, well, they never come around here. Not unless they're following something, anyway.' She scanned the sea between the mermaids' reef and the rocky island. It was calm with just a few waves breaking in white ripples. She was sure she could easily swim out to the island. 'I'd be fine. I could get there and back no problem.'

'No,' Sam told her. 'You'll get into trouble. You mustn't go!'

Electra sighed. *You mustn't* were words she seemed to hear every day at the moment. *You mustn't* dive off the high rocks; *you mustn't* go swimming into the deep caves; *you mustn't* swim outside the reef. It wasn't fair. Sometimes it seemed like she wasn't allowed to do anything exciting at all. She hadn't minded so much when she was little. Then it had been fun to stay near Mermaid Island and play in the safe waters, but now she was nine she longed to go exploring.

'I *want* to go,' she protested. 'It's boring here.' She looked around at the sharp coral reef that circled Mermaid Island. It jutted out of the sea and acted as a barrier, keeping out any dangerous sea creatures. Only adult merpeople were allowed to swim through the gate and out into the deep sea, but they hardly ever did. Most of the time they stayed happily in the peaceful turquoise waters near their island, talking, laughing, swimming with the sea horses, fish, dolphins

and other sea creatures that they shared their lives with. Merpeople didn't like exploring. They liked staying out of sight, safely hidden from curious humans.

But Electra wasn't like most merpeople. She longed for adventure.

'You know,' she said, looking at the rocky island out at sea again, 'I think a sea fairy lives over there.'

'A sea fairy,' Sam and Sasha echoed.

Electra nodded. She wasn't sure she really believed in sea fairies any more, but she knew that the twins, who were a year younger than her, did. 'If I went I might meet her.' She looked at the twins. 'We could all go together,' she suggested. 'I bet the sea fairy would grant us a wish – and maybe some fairy food.'

Sam and Sasha almost looked tempted.

'Sea fairies make magic sweets,' Electra went on, trying to persuade them. 'Sugar sea horses that change flavour in your mouth and tiny starfish that explode like sherbet when you eat them.'

'Magic sweets,' sighed Sasha, twisting her long blonde plait.

'And wishes,' said Sam longingly.

For a moment, Electra thought they might actually agree to come with her, but then Sam shook his head. 'It's too dangerous,' he said, looking at his sister. 'We can't. Dad would be cross with us.'

Sasha nodded.

Electra sighed in frustration and made up her mind. 'Then I'll go on my own.' She dived into the water.

'No!' Sasha exclaimed, following her down. 'Electra! Don't!'

'I won't be long,' Electra said, searching for a gap in the coral wall.

'Make up an excuse if Mum comes to find me.'

'But what shall we say?' Sasha gasped.

'Anything!' Electra found a space in the wall and quickly squeezed through, trying not to scratch herself on the sharp pink coral. As she bobbed up in the water on the other side of the reef, she grinned at Sam and Sasha's alarmed faces. 'I'll say hi to the sea fairy for you!' she said, and then she plunged excitedly away into the deep sea.

Chapter Two

Electra found the water much colder away from the safety of the reef. The waves splashed roughly against her face and she quickly dived beneath the surface. It was easier to swim deep down in the ocean, but it was also dark and spooky. It wasn't at all like swimming in the warm water round Mermaid Island. The deep sea was full of shadows and strange moving shapes. As Electra peered through the gloom, something caught round her legs.

She gasped and kicked hard. A harmless rope of seaweed floated away. Her heart pounded. She'd thought it was an electric eel. She paused. Maybe she should go back.

But then what would Sam and Sasha say if she returned so quickly? *No*, she decided, *I'm not going to turn round. Now I'm here I'm going to have an adventure.*

She swam on, wishing for about the millionth time in her life that she were a faster swimmer. But being adventurous wasn't the only way in which Electra was different from the other merpeople on Mermaid Island. She wasn't like them in another way as well. All the other merpeople had long silver tails, but, instead, she had two legs. She knew it was because she had been born a human and not a merperson. Every night, her mermaid mum, Maris, told her the story of how she had come to live on Mermaid Island. It was Electra's favourite tale and, as she kicked through the dark water, she could almost hear her mum's low musical voice in her ear.

'One night, eight years ago, there was a dreadful storm. All night long, the lightning flashed and the thunder crashed and the rain poured down. In the morning, when we came out of our caves, we saw a small boat

floating across the deep ocean just outside the reef. It was the sort of boat that humans use when they are trying to escape from a sinking ship. Everyone thought it was empty, but I thought I heard a strange noise so I swam through the reef and went over to it.' At that point in the story, Electra's mum usually smiled. 'And you know what I found?'

It was the moment Electra always waited for. 'Me!'

'Yes, you,' her mum would say. 'You were just a baby. Kicking away with fat pink legs and gurgling at the blue sky. As soon as you saw me you smiled and laughed. I scooped you up and took you back to the island where we gave you some sea powder so that you could breathe under the water. That was how you came to live with the merpeople instead of humans. You became my daughter and I named you Electra and we've been together ever since.'

Electra loved the story. It made her feel different and special. 'My gift from the sea,' her mum often called her. At least she did when she wasn't telling Electra off for getting into trouble.

Electra sighed. She always seemed to be getting into trouble these days! All her friends, the other mergirls and merboys, seemed very happy just swimming around near the island, playing on the reef and going to their lessons, but Electra had started to find the reef really boring. She wanted more. She wanted excitement.

Like this, she thought determinedly as she swam through the spooky water.

A shadow loomed up ahead. Electra bobbed up to the surface. She was almost at the mysterious island. The rocks round it were sharp and dangerous, and a dark cloud hung over them.

Electra swallowed nervously, but she was determined to go and explore the island. She scanned the rocks and saw a gap that she could get through. Judging her moment, she waited until she felt a particularly large wave coming and then she plunged into it and let it carry her between the rocks. She landed on a small sandy beach. Shaking the water out of her hair and smoothing down her pink and purple seaweed bikini, she stood up and looked around.

Chapter Three

The island seemed much less creepy now that Electra was standing on it. The rocks that had looked so black and menacing from the sea were actually just a dull grey, and here and there small purple flowers grew on ledges. Feeling braver, Electra began to explore. Perhaps she would find a sea fairy after all. She smiled as she imagined what Sam and Sasha would say if she did. They would be so jealous!

'Hello?' she called out. 'Hello? Is there anyone here?' There was no reply.

There were a few small caves but to her disappointment they

were all empty. Holding on tightly to the rocks, she climbed round the island. Reaching the far side, she saw another little beach. She stopped. There was a grey shape lying on the sand.

It moved and suddenly she saw that it had a tail and a blunt snout and a grey fin. It was a baby dolphin!

Forgetting all about sea fairies, Electra scrambled over the rocks.

When he saw her approaching, the dolphin tried to get away, but he was stranded out of the water on the beach. His tail flapped helplessly. His black eyes looked at her in alarm.

'Do you want some help?' Electra asked quickly.

The dolphin struggled even more, his face full of fear as he looked at her legs.

Suddenly Electra realized that he must think she was a human. She quickly changed to Dolphin language, a series of whistles and squeaks that all merpeople could speak. 'Do you need to get back into the water?' she asked him.

The dolphin stopped flapping his fins and looked at her in surprise. 'You speak Dolphin?'

Electra nodded.

'I . . . I've never met a human who could speak Dolphin before,' the dolphin said nervously.

Electra laughed. 'But I'm not a human. I'm a mermaid.' She saw the dolphin look at her legs in astonishment.

'It's a long story,' she said. She crouched down beside him. 'So, what's your name?'

'Splash,' the dolphin replied.

'Well, I'm Electra.' Electra looked round. 'Would you like me to help you get back into the sea?' She knew that dolphins shouldn't stay out of the water for long.

'Yes, please,' Splash said gratefully. 'I got washed up here. I was swimming past and I didn't realize the current would be so strong. I just got swept on to the beach.'

Electra began to push the dolphin

back towards the water. His skin felt firm and smooth.

'Thanks,' Splash said, trying to help by wriggling.

Electra gave him a last push down the sand and he slithered into the sea. She plunged into the water beside him.

They swam away from the rocks. Splash leapt out of the water in delight. He swam underneath Electra and then bobbed up, his snout appearing beside her. 'Wow! It feels good to be back in the sea again,' he said, clicking his tongue. His eyes danced merrily. 'Tag!' he said, touching her with his snout. 'Bet you can't catch me!'

He turned and swam away.

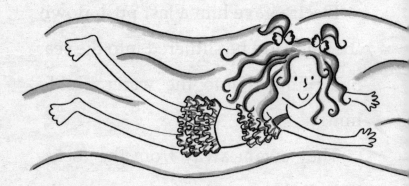

Electra raced after him. But he was so fast, there was no way she could tag him back. Splash slipped this way and that, avoiding her outstretched hands.

'I give up!' she gasped, giggling. 'You're too quick for me.'

Splash swam over to her and butted his head softly against hers. 'You're fun. Can we be friends?'

'Of course,' Electra said. She glanced around. 'Where's your mum?' Baby dolphins nearly always had their mums nearby.

Splash suddenly looked very sad.

'She died a week ago,' he said, blinking. 'She . . . she was killed by two sharks.'

'By sharks!' Electra exclaimed in horror.

Splash nodded. 'I only just escaped.'

Electra felt a prickle of fear. Of course she'd heard stories about how vicious sharks were, with their sharp teeth and their love of hunting, but the reef round Mermaid Island kept sharks out and it was easy to forget what dangerous creatures they were. She looked around at the sea, realizing just how alone she and

Splash were. Maybe it wasn't such a good idea being out in the deep water. If a shark came now . . .

'Look, why don't you come back to Mermaid Island with me?' she said quickly to Splash. 'There are other dolphins there. The merpeople adopt baby dolphins who have been orphaned and look after them until they are old enough to go back out to sea.' Her blue eyes lit up. 'Maybe my mum will adopt you and you can come and live with us in our cave.'

'I'd like that!' Splash exclaimed.

'Me too,' Electra said eagerly. 'Come on then. Let's go back to the island!'

Swimming side by side, they set off through the sea.

Chapter Four

Electra and Splash headed straight for Mermaid Island. 'So, how did you escape from the sharks?' Electra asked curiously.

'I swam and swam,' Splash told her. 'The sharks chased after me but I got away. I hope they don't come here. They've been following me all week.'

Feeling a prickle of fear, Electra glanced around, almost expecting to see two black fins cutting through the water. But the sea was empty. Still, even just knowing that there were two sharks out there hunting Splash down made her feel very nervous. She started to swim as fast as she could. The reef was still a long way off.

Splash seemed to feel just as worried. He nudged her with his snout. 'Shall we go faster?' he suggested.

'I can't,' Electra told him, her breath coming in short gasps. 'I'm swimming as quickly as I can. It's hard without a tail!'

They swam and swam. At long last the pink coral rose up in front of them.

Electra felt a rush of relief. They had made it! She was surprised to see that Sam and Sasha weren't watching out for her to come back. She frowned. Where were they?

She put the thought to the back of her mind. Sam and Sasha had probably just gone home for lunch and right now she had a more urgent problem to think about. She had to work out how she was going to get Splash into the safe waters of Mermaid Island. There was no way he would fit through the hole in the reef that she had squeezed through.

There *was* a gate but only the grown-ups were allowed to use that. If she tried to take him through it then everyone would see she had been out in the deep sea and then she would really be in trouble!

'I'm not sure how I'm going to get you into the sea inside the reef,' she told Splash. 'I can't use the gate because I'm not supposed to be out here.'

'No problem,' Splash said with a flip of his tail. 'I'll just jump over the coral.'

'Jump over!' Electra said in

astonishment. She'd never seen anyone jump over the reef before.

Splash nodded. 'I'm good at jumping. I'll be able to do it easily. You go in first and I'll follow.'

Electra dived through the hole in the wall and bobbed up to the surface just in time to see Splash taking off and flying like a silver streak through the air.

 He plunged safely into the water beside her.

'I told you I could do it!' he said, surfacing and opening his mouth in a huge dolphin grin.

Electra breathed out a sigh of relief. It had been a good adventure, but she was glad it was over.

'So, where do we go now?' Splash asked, looking around curiously.

'Now,' Electra said, 'you come and meet my mum and we ask her if she'll adopt you. Come on. Our cave is this way!'

Chapter Five

Electra dived down through the warm blue water. Splash followed. They swam through shoals of multicoloured rainbow fish and past a group of darting sea horses, down to where the merpeople's caves were hollowed out of the coral near the seabed.

'That's my school over there,' Electra said, pointing out a large cave with rows of benches made out of rock outside it. 'That's where we sit when we're having lessons, but we're on holiday at the moment.'

'What sorts of lessons do you do?' Splash asked curiously.

Electra shrugged. 'Oh, just normal things. We have diving, jewellery making, hairdressing and underwater gardening. We also study rocks and shells and learn about other sea creatures. It's all quite boring.' Suddenly she remembered something and her face lit up. 'But next term Miss Solon, our teacher, is going to show us how to collect mermaid fire for cooking with and heating things up. I can't wait. It's the first proper magic we get to do.'

They swam on past the school and past the row of small shops that sold sweets, gardening tools, shell jewellery and hair accessories. Then they weaved in and out of the fronds of green and purple seaweed until they reached the underwater cave where

Electra lived with her mum. Outside the cave was a neat garden of sea lettuces, pink and lilac sea anemones and rocks covered in yellow and red flower-shaped sea squirts. The nearby cave entrance was hung with a curtain of cockleshells that swayed in the currents of water.

'Mum! I'm home!' Electra called.

Maris, her mum, was inside the cave, setting out silvery plates on the rocky table for lunch. Her long red hair was caught back with a string of tiny brown-and-white cowrie shells. Electra loved the fact that she and Maris both had red hair. It made Maris adopting her seem even more perfect.

'Hi, sweetheart.' Maris stared in

surprise as she saw Splash. 'There's
. . . there's a dolphin with you,
Electra!'

Splash stood upright and clapped
his fins politely in greeting.

'This is Splash, Mum,' Electra
explained. 'I found him on . . .' she
trailed off as suddenly she realized
that saying she had found Splash on
the rocky island out at sea might not
be a good plan. 'I just found him,' she
said hastily. 'His mother has died and
he needs someone to look after him.
Can we keep him, Mum?'

Maris sighed. 'Oh, Electra. We

haven't got the space for a dolphin.'

'He won't need much room,' Electra protested.

Maris shook her head. 'No, I'm sorry, sweetheart. It's just going to be too much work and our cave is small enough as it is.' She looked at Splash. 'You can stay for lunch, Splash, and then we'll have to take you to the dolphin sanctuary this afternoon. I'm sorry we can't have you here, but I'm sure they'll be able to find you a good home.'

'But Splash is my friend, Mum,' Electra said as Splash looked sadly at her. 'Oh, please can he stay?'

'The answer's no, I'm afraid,' Maris replied. She spoke kindly but firmly. 'Now, lunch will be ready in fifteen minutes. Why don't you two go and play until then?'

Electra went over to Splash and stroked him. 'I'm sorry,' she said as they swam out of the cave.

'It's OK,' Splash whistled bravely, but Electra could tell he was upset.

Just then, Ronan, the twins' father, came swimming out of the next-door cave. He was a tall merman with thick white-blond hair like the twins. He had a piece of paper in his hand and he looked worried.

'Electra? Are Sam and Sasha with you?' he asked.

'No,' Electra replied in surprise. She'd thought the twins must have swum home for lunch.

'That's odd,' Ronan said, frowning.

'I've just found this note. It's very strange.'

Electra swam over curiously. 'What does it say?'

Ronan held the note out and Electra read:

Dear Dad

We'll be back soon. We're going to look for a sea fairy and have an adventure! We're with Electra so don't worry.

Love from Sam and Sasha.

Ronan shook his head. 'Gone on an adventure. What do they mean? And why do they say they're with you? They're obviously not.'

Electra felt as if her stomach had just dropped to her toes. The twins had gone on an adventure to find a sea fairy! That could only mean one thing: they'd decided to swim out to the rocky island after her. Just where two sharks might be!

Ronan swam off. 'Sasha! Sam!' he called, searching for the twins.

'What's the matter?' Splash asked, looking at Electra's horrified face.

'It's my friends,' Electra told him. 'I said I was going to the island to see a sea fairy and now they've decided to go too.'

'But the two sharks that have been following me might be out there!' Splash exclaimed.

'I know,' Electra said, her heart beating fast. 'Look, you stay here. I'm going to go after them.'

Without waiting for an answer, she headed towards the surface. She had to go and warn the twins of the danger they were in!

Chapter Six

Electra squeezed out through the reef and looked out across the sea. Her sharp blue eyes caught sight of two heads bobbing up and down near the rocky cliffs of the island. It was Sam and Sasha.

Kicking hard, Electra set off after them.

She swam as fast as she could, but the twins, with their tails, could swim much quicker than her and with every second that passed they just seemed to get further and further away. Electra felt like sobbing in frustration.

Suddenly a grey shape swooshed into the water just in front of her.

'Splash!' Electra cried, stopping in surprise. 'What are you doing?'

'I want to help,' Splash said. 'You saved me, Electra, when I was stranded on the beach. Now it's my turn to help you.'

'But it might be dangerous,' Electra gasped, continuing to swim through the rough sea. 'Those sharks might come.'

'I don't care,' Splash answered. 'Hold on to my fin and I'll pull you through the water. You'll reach your friends much faster that way.'

Electra stared at him. It was a brilliant idea! 'OK,' she said, grabbing his fin with both hands. 'Thanks, Splash!'

Splash surged forward. Foam dashed against Electra's face as Splash raced through the water. She coughed and spluttered and tried to peer through her sea-spattered eyelashes. She had never been so fast. If it hadn't been for the waves splashing up around her she would have thought she was flying.

In almost no time at all, the rocky island loomed up out of the water in front of them. Splash slowed slightly and, shaking her hair out of her eyes,

Electra saw her friends.

'Sam! Sasha!' she cried.

The twins turned. 'Electra!' they said in astonishment.

Sam stared. 'Who's the dolphin?'

'I'll tell you later,' Electra said quickly. 'There's no time now. You've got to turn round! There might be sharks nearby.'

'Sharks!' Sam echoed.

'They're looking for me,' Splash

told them. 'They've been following me all week.'

'Come on, we've got to get out of here,' Electra told the twins.

Sam and Sasha didn't need any more persuading. With a swish of their tails, they turned and began to swim swiftly back to Mermaid Island.

'How did you know we were out here?' Sam asked as he swam.

'I saw the note you left your dad,' Electra said, hanging on to Splash's fin so she could keep up with them.

'We waited and waited for you but

you were so long we thought you must have found a fairy,' Sasha said. 'So, we decided to come after you. *Did* you find a fairy?'

'No,' Electra said. 'I found Splash instead. His mum was killed last week by two sharks.'

'The ones who are chasing him?' Sam asked.

Electra nodded. The twins looked pale and speeded up even more.

Just then Splash whistled in alarm. 'Help! They're here!'

Electra glanced round and her blood seemed to freeze. Two sinister fins were nosing through the water near the island. It was the sharks! They'd arrived!

'Come on,' she gasped. 'They don't seem to have seen us yet. Keep swimming! We're not that far from the reef now.'

The sharks stopped. There was a horrible pause and then they started to swim swiftly towards the twins and Electra. They moved like deadly arrows through the water, their fins cutting through the waves.

'They've spotted us!' Electra shrieked in alarm. *'Swim!'*

Chapter Seven

Sam and Sasha plunged through the water, their silvery tails swishing back and forth.

'Hold on tight!' Splash cried to Electra.

She didn't need to be told. She

grasped his fin and kicked with all her might. Splash surged forward, overtaking the twins.

Electra looked desperately towards Mermaid Island. They were close now but were they close enough? She could see some of the adult merpeople looking out over the coral reef towards them. She recognized Ronan and her mum. Their faces were very alarmed.

Glancing behind her, she saw why. The sharks were closing in on Sam and Sasha. The twins were both fast swimmers, but they weren't fast enough to outswim two sharks. Electra saw the horrible creatures opening their mouths, their beady eyes gleaming.

She knew she had to do something. It was all her fault Sam and Sasha were there. If she hadn't tried to persuade them to have an adventure they'd be safely sitting down to lunch now.

'Splash!' she shouted desperately through the spray of the water. 'I've got to go back. The sharks are going to catch the twins! You go on!'

'No,' Splash said. 'Not without you.' He swung round and they raced back towards Sam and Sasha.

'What are you doing?' Sam gasped in surprise.

'It doesn't matter. Just keep swimming!' Electra yelled. Her heart was pounding in her chest.

'Um . . . what now, Electra?' Splash asked uncertainly.

Electra didn't know what to say. She'd come back to the twins without a plan in mind and now she couldn't think of anything to do. The sharks were getting closer and closer. She *had* to think of something! Suddenly a floating rope of seaweed brushed against her leg. It gave her an idea.

'Quick!' she cried. She grabbed the seaweed rope with one hand. It was very long and tough. 'I've got a plan, Splash. We can use this seaweed.' Keeping her eyes on the approaching sharks, she gabbled out her idea.

'All right,' Splash agreed once she finished. 'Here goes!'

He began to swim straight towards the sharks. Holding tight, Electra saw the sharks hesitate. Their black eyes moved between the twins

who were swimming away and the dolphin and mermaid who were swimming straight towards them.

Please, she thought desperately, *please let this work!*

To her relief, the sharks acted just as she hoped. Forgetting about the twins, they began to head eagerly to meet her and Splash, their fins snaking through the water.

With her heart in her mouth, Electra pulled herself on to Splash's smooth back. Her knees gripped his slippery sides and she clutched the thick seaweed rope. She knew she mustn't let it go.

'Now!' Electra cried to Splash as the sharks reached them. Splash leapt into the air. As he soared over the sharks' backs, Electra let the seaweed rope fall. She held on tight to one end as Splash plunged into the water on the other side. It was hard to stay on him but she clung to his fin with all her might. Diving underneath the sharks' grey bellies, he leapt out of the water again and over their backs. Electra saw the bewilderment and confusion in the sharks' tiny eyes. She knew they couldn't understand what was going on. In their world, dolphins and mermaids were supposed to swim away from them, not jump over them.

'Again!' she shouted as Splash plunged into the water for a second time. The seaweed rope was now wrapped round the two sharks and as Splash dived out of the water, Electra pulled the rope as hard as she could. Feeling it tighten round them, the sharks started to panic and swim round and round but the more they swam the more tangled up in the rope they became.

Electra knew the seaweed rope wouldn't be strong enough to hold them for long. She glanced towards the reef. To her relief she saw that Sam and Sasha had reached it. Their father was helping them across it. They were safe!

'Let's go!' she shouted to Splash.

Splash didn't need to be told twice. Turning swiftly, he raced towards the coral.

Electra looked back. The sharks had broken free from the rope and were coming after them. They looked mad with anger as they swept through the water.

'Quick!' she cried in fear.

The reef was approaching fast. Electra could hear the sharks snapping behind them. There was going to be no time to find the hole for her to squeeze through.

Splash seemed to have realized it too.

'Hold on!' he cried. He tensed and Electra knew he was going to jump. She clung on tightly to his fin. He soared into the air. For a moment the blue sky seemed to spin round them and then they were plunging downwards. Down, down into the safe turquoise water of Mermaid Island.

As the water closed over her head, Electra lost her grip and tumbled free. Moments later, she surfaced, shaking the water out of her eyes. 'Wow!' she gasped in relief as Splash bobbed up beside her. 'That was amazing!'

'We're safe!' Splash cried.

'And it's all thanks to you,' Electra said, hugging him shakily.

'Electra!' Electra swung round. Her mum was swimming towards her. She looked very, very angry.

'Uh-oh,' Electra muttered to Splash, her heart sinking.

'Whatever do you think you're doing going out on the sea like that?'

Maris cried, her face pale. 'Of all the stupid things to do . . .'

'Maris, please!' Ronan swam suddenly between them, an arm round each of the twins. 'Electra saved Sam and Sasha's lives. Please don't be angry with her. She was so brave.' He looked at Electra. 'Thank you, Electra.'

Electra looked anxiously at her mum.

Maris's face suddenly crumpled and her eyes filled with tears. 'Oh, sweetheart. I was just so worried.' She swam forward and the next moment Electra found herself being smothered in a huge hug. 'I thought you were going to be killed.'

'I'm OK, Mum,' Electra said. She wriggled free. 'I'm fine.'

'My brave girl,' Maris said, shaking her head. 'I'm so glad you're safe – that you're *all* safe,' she said, looking at the twins.

'You were amazing, Electra,' Sam said admiringly.

'We'd have been eaten if it hadn't been for you,' Sasha agreed.

Electra glanced across at Splash. 'Well, I couldn't have done it without Splash. He was fantastic!'

Splash looked down at the water and Electra knew that if dolphins could blush, his face would have 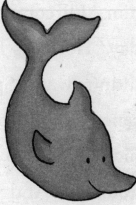 been bright pink. She stroked him. 'Thank you,' she said softly.

Splash nudged her with his snout. 'That's OK. I'm just glad I could help.' He hesitated. 'Electra, will . . . will you still be my friend even when I'm at the dolphin sanctuary?' he asked uncertainly.

'Of course I will!' Electra kissed him. 'I'll come and visit you every day.' Her eyes filled with tears. She didn't want Splash to go to the sanctuary. 'I'll bring you all sorts of nice things to eat,' she told him quickly. 'And I'll take you out swimming.'

Splash swallowed. 'I'd really like

that.' He spoke bravely but he looked really upset.

Maris looked from him to Electra. 'Splash, you know I said we couldn't adopt you?'

Splash nodded sadly.

'Well, I've changed my mind.' Maris grinned suddenly. 'How would you like to come and live with us after all?'

Splash whistled in delight. 'Come and live with you? I'd love to!'

Electra stared at her mum. 'But you said we didn't have room.'

'We'll manage,' replied Maris.

'That's brilliant, Mum!' Electra cried. 'Did you hear that, Splash? You can stay with us forever. Well, at least until you're older and want to go back to the deep sea.'

Splash butted his head against Electra's chest and looked at her with loving dark eyes. 'I'll never want that, Electra.'

Electra hugged him. 'Me neither,' she said with a huge smile.

Not Quite a Mermaid

Linda Chapman

You don't need a tail to make a splash!

Electra is different from other mermaids.
She has legs instead of a tail and is always getting
into scrapes in search of adventure!

Electra's class is having a competition to collect magic mermaid
fire from the seabed – the deeper you dive, the more you can find.
Will Electra and Splash be brave enough to dive to the very bottom?

puffin.co.uk